For Annabelle, Farah, Ar
Lottie, Lyra and Jago

The **Global Travels** *of* **Simon, Katie** *and* **The Cloud**

Chapters 1&2
OXFORDSHIRE

Chapter
BR

Chapter 12
NEW YORK

Chapter 13
BACK TO OXFORDSHIRE

Cha
ON T

Chapter 11
RIO DE JANEIRO

CAPE HORN

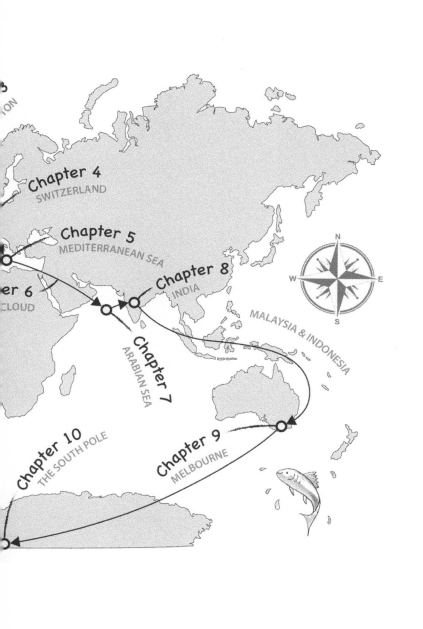

Chapter 4
SWITZERLAND

Chapter 5
MEDITERRANEAN SEA

Chapter 8
INDIA

er 6
CLOUD

Chapter 7
ARABIAN SEA

MALAYSIA & INDONESIA

Chapter 10
THE SOUTH POLE

Chapter 9
MELBOURNE

N
W   E
S

CONTENTS

CHAPTER 1

SIMON AND KATIE MEET THE BIG CLOUD

Simon and his sister Katie were quite ordinary children, but extraordinary things seemed to keep happening to them. Such as their adventure on the Big Cloud.

They were walking across the field near their home one day when they looked up and saw a huge cloud in the sky. It looked as if it were made of big cushions of cotton wool.

'I wish I could roll about on that,' said Simon.

'So do I,' said Katie.

Suddenly, to their great surprise, they saw a boy standing on the edge of the cloud. He was waving to them.

'How did he get up there?' wondered Simon.

'Perhaps he flew up,' said Katie.

Simon was about to tell Katie not to be silly, but then he thought about it for a moment. It didn't really seem very likely, but then neither did seeing a boy standing on a cloud.

Then the most remarkable thing you could ever imagine happened.

The boy took an armful of cloud and blew into it, making it look like a parachute. Then he took some more cloud and made it into a kind of basket. He fastened it by some cloud threads to the parachute, jumped in and began to sail down to them.

In a moment, his wonderful cloud balloon had brought him gently down to the field where they were walking.

He was a nice boy with blue eyes and hair that was a bit gingery. He wore a yellow T-shirt, and bits of white cloud had stuck to his clothes and hair.

Suddenly, to their great surprise, they saw a boy standing on the edge of the cloud,
he was waving to them.

'Hello,' he said, stepping out of the cloud basket. 'I'm Sam.'

'Hello,' said Simon. He was rather nervous because he felt sure Sam was going to ask them to get into the cloud basket and go sailing up into the sky, and he certainly didn't want Katie to think that he might be afraid.

As it happened, Katie was thinking the same thing. It did seem a very long way up to the Big Cloud.

'Well,' said Sam, 'don't let's mess about. I came to tell you it is your turn to be the Cloud Children.'

'The what?' gasped Simon and Katie together.

'The Cloud Children.'

'Who are they? And what exactly do they do?' asked Simon.

'They ride on the clouds for a year. And they help people who need helping.'

'But we have to go in for tea soon,' said Simon.

'I'm very hungry,' Katie put in.

Katie was often very hungry.

'Oh, don't worry,' replied Sam. 'Once you are on the Big Cloud, time stands still. You can go all the way round the world and still be back here in time for tea today.'

Simon and Katie looked at each other and started to laugh, but they soon realised that Sam was serious.

'But I'm hungry now,' exclaimed Katie. 'I can't wait a year for my tea.'

Sam laughed. 'Come and have some cloud tea.'

'Crumbs,' said Simon. 'Hadn't we better fetch our coats?'

'No need for coats. It's very warm up there usually – except over the North Pole,' said Sam.

Simon was looking thoughtful. 'How did you come to pick us to be the Cloud Children?' he asked.

'I don't really know that,' admitted Sam. 'You just get a message from the Cloud – or from the sky. And then you just know which brother and sister will be the best to be the Cloud Children.'

Simon and Katie felt very proud that they were the best.

'The Cloud goes by magic time,' said Sam, 'so, although it will seem to take you a year to go around the world, your mum won't even know you've been. So far as she is concerned, you will be back for tea today.'

'Wow,' said Simon and Katie together.

'Hop in,' said Sam.

The parachute was a bit floppy, so Sam told them to blow hard into it. It filled out like a great balloon. In a moment they were whizzing up into the sky. The houses, roads and cars, trees, farms and cows, schools and churches, ponds and rivers, villages and towns began to look smaller and smaller. The cloud basket was very comfortable, and Simon and Katie were not at all frightened.

A black crow sailed past them and looked surprised. 'Afternoon,' he cawed in a croaky voice.

In ten minutes they had caught the Big Cloud up.

'All aboard,' shouted Sam as they came alongside, and they all jumped onto the Cloud. It was like jumping onto a trampoline. You bounced up and down for a while, and then you rolled about as if the Cloud were all made of soft springy cushions. It was a bit like the bouncy castle Katie had had at her last birthday party.

Simon jumped up as high as he could, came down on the Cloud, then shot ten feet into the air again.

'Cool!' he shouted. 'It's like being a giant.'

'Mind you don't fall off,' called Sam. 'If you do, grab a bit of cloud and it will act like a parachute. Then, if you blow into it, it will bring you up again.'

The place where they had landed was a kind of plain made of cloud tops like big white mushrooms. The rest of the Big Cloud towered up in great banks and peaks, some of which were snowy white, and others coloured gold or red or purple by the afternoon sun.

'Meet my sister,' said Sam.

A girl of Katie's age was striding towards them. At first, she seemed quite small because she came from a golden, warm-looking corner of the Cloud quite a long way off, under a mountain. But she took enormous steps from cloudy mushroom top to cloudy mushroom top. In fact, she bounced towards them.

'I'm Margaret,' she said. 'Hello.'

4

They said hello. Then Sam turned to Simon and Katie. 'We'll show you how to make tea and where the food is. And where you'll be nice and warm at night, of course. Then we'll have to be off. We have to be home soon. We live on a farm, and I think I can just see it coming up.' He pointed to some very distant fields and woods.

They all strode off with huge strides towards the nice warm corner of the mountain. Katie fell down once or twice and came up with little bits of frilly cloud in her hair, but it was great fun bouncing along like a ball.

When they got there both Simon and Katie looked very worried. 'Where's the food?' they asked.

Sam laughed. 'The Cloud provides everything,' he said mysteriously.

While Margaret was shaping some cloud into a table and making big cushions to sit on, Sam asked, 'What would you like to drink? Lemonade?'

'Yes, please,' said Simon and Katie together.

Sam took two bits of ordinary cloud and shaped them into tumblers. Then he scooped two bits of golden, sunny cloud into his hands, squeezed them into the tumblers and handed them to Simon and Katie.

'Lemonade,' he said, smiling.

'Super,' said Simon, guzzling it down. 'Can we have some more, please?' So they all had another tumblerful.

'Now, what would you like for tea?' asked Sam.

'Bacon and chips, please,' said Simon.

'Me too, please,' said Katie.

Simon thought that perhaps Sam would not be able to make that out of the Cloud.

But he did. He quickly flattened out two cloud plates. Then he took some huge strides to halfway up a cliff, where the sun was shining golden on one part and purply-red on another.

He took out a penknife and cut a pile of golden chips onto each plate. Then he shaved some rashers of bacon from the purply cloud and popped both plates into a special cloud oven on a ledge in the sun.

In a moment, they were all smelling that wonderful smell of sizzling bacon.

'There you are,' Sam said triumphantly. 'Bacon and chips.'

Munch, scrunch, munch. Those were the only sounds to be heard for ten minutes while Katie and Simon ate their tea.

'You said we were to help people,' said Simon through a mouthful of chips. 'How do we do that?'

'Well, I had better explain,' said Sam. 'This is one of the Big Clouds. There are quite a few clouds like this floating around the world – about a hundred, I should think. And each one has a brother and sister on it. They are like a secret army. The children on them may be American or African, French, Arab or West Indian, or English, like you. From any country. You all have to keep a good look out down below. If you see any bad things being done, you have to try to stop them and put things right. If you see anyone who needs help, then you help them.'

'But how can we see them?' asked Simon. His tummy kept rumbling. He had eaten too many cloud chips.

'Make yourself a pair of binoculars like this,' and Sam scooped out two cloud tubes with his fingers and held them to his eyes. 'You will find you can see the smallest little thing on the earth quite clearly. Try them.'

Simon took them and then let out a great shout of surprise. A house that had looked like a small box to his ordinary eyesight was so big through the cloud binoculars that he could see into the dining room window. He could also see a lady at the door looking round anxiously. He could even see a bumblebee on a flower near her hand.

He told Sam.

'Oh, that will be our mum,' said Sam. 'It's incredible. We have had lots of adventures and been a year on the magic cloud. But for Mum it's still teatime on the day we left. We'll have to hop off here.'

He told Simon that if he put the cloud tube to his ear, he would be able to hear what Sam's mum was saying.

Simon did so. The voice came up to him as if through a radio: 'Sammy, Margaret, where are you? Tea's ready.'

6

Katie had a listen too. It made them feel rather homesick to see Sam and his sister going back to their farm, but they looked their bravest.

'Don't worry,' shouted Sam, as they climbed into the parachute basket, 'you'll have a wonderful time. You can't stop wars and big things, of course. Just try to do as many little things to help people as you can.'

'We'll try,' Simon shouted to them as they began to float down.

'Yes, we'll try,' echoed Katie.

They both felt rather sad and hoped their mother would not miss them. But what an incredible adventure to happen to you when you are just strolling across a field. And everything was so exciting but so comfortable. And it did seem as if the Big Cloud was humming to itself happily at having them aboard.

CHAPTER 2

THE RESCUE OF TIMOTHY TUMBLES

It was an hour later. The Cloud was sailing along. The sun was setting, and all the top slopes of the cloud mountain were coloured in beautiful shades of gold and orange and purple and red.

But it was getting rather chilly, and both Simon and Katie began to think of home. A moment later Katie began to cry.

'I want my mummy,' she shouted in a very loud voice that made some bits of the Cloud shake like jelly. 'I want my nice warm bed and Snoopy to cuddle up to.'

'Oh, don't be silly,' said Simon.

'You're always telling me not to be silly,' cried Katie.

'That's because you are silly,' said Simon unkindly. Of course, this is always the way that elder brothers talk to younger sisters and elder sisters talk to younger brothers.

Simon, as leader of the adventure, had been busy making a bed out of the Cloud.

'Come here and snuggle down under the cloud blanket I have made, Katie,' he said more kindly.

He quite liked Katie really. It was a pity, of course, that she had to be a girl.

Katie climbed onto the cloud bed beside him and slid sulkily beneath the fluffy cover. It was lovely and warm.

She thought, *Simon is quite nice really. Except that he's a boy.*

'Want some jelly?' asked Simon suddenly.

Katie was nice and warm now, so she said yes please.

Simon bounded out of bed and leapt up the cloud mountain with great strides until he came to a part that was coloured a beautiful pink. It was actually still quivering from Katie's sobs. That, of course, made it all the more jellified.

Simon scooped out two large portions onto two cloud plates and went back to Katie. They munched away, dissolving the jelly in their mouths, while still sitting in their bed.

Then Simon said, 'I'd better go and look to see if there are any bad things going on down on earth.'

When he said 'down on earth' it made Katie feel all funny inside – although, of course, the jelly made her feel a bit wobbly too. She realised suddenly that they were really sailing through the sky on a cloud – a very special cloud – hundreds of feet above the ground. She had forgotten about that for a while.

Simon bounced off towards the edge. He felt rather important and big-headed. But the Cloud very soon put him right about that. As he zoomed along, he bounced into a big hole where the Cloud was golden even though the sun was not shining on it. He climbed out again, covered in bits of golden cloud.

'Mm. Yum yum,' he said to himself. He licked the bits of cloud off his lips and tried hard to get at a bit that had stuck to the end of his nose.

'Mm, yum,' he said to himself again. 'Tastes of custard.'

That was because he had just fallen into the custard-flavoured cloud hole. The Cloud had wanted to slow him up a bit so that he did not fall off the edge. But the Cloud had also thought that it would be rather nice to show him the custard supply on the way.

At the very edge of the Cloud Simon made himself some binoculars and looked down.

Suddenly Katie saw him jumping up and down furiously. He was shouting something, but she could not tell what he was saying. So she made a little cloud tube and put it to her ear. It worked like magic.

'You are a horrible, nasty, wicked man,' she heard Simon shouting. 'You beastly, cruel, horrible, nasty man. You are a nasty, beastly, cruel, horrible man.'

Evidently Simon could not think of any words bad enough for the man he was looking at.

Then, 'You leave that poor dog alone. Do you hear me? You should never ever hit dogs. Or any animals.'

Katie leapt out of her cloud bed and rushed towards him so fast that she nearly bounced over the edge.

Fortunately, the clouds that take the Secret Army of Children around the world doing good things are very special clouds. The Big Clouds, as they are called, are very careful to look after the children and keep them safe.

And so it was that when Katie came to the edge too fast, the cloud caused a little swirl and brought a bank of cloud cushion up in front of her to bounce her back to safety.

'Do be careful,' Simon said. 'You mustn't rush about so, Katie.'

'You fell into that hole because you were rushing about like King Simon,' Katie accused him, 'and anyway, you smell of custard.'

'Well, never mind about that,' said Simon, who felt a bit embarrassed about smelling of custard. 'Just have a look through the binoculars and see what that horrible, cruel, nasty, beastly man is doing to his dog.'

Katie looked. Far down below, in the back garden of a cottage, a man was standing over a small, ginger-brown, fuzzy-haired dog.

'He's been hitting him!' cried Simon. 'Come on, down we go.'

And before Katie could quite make up her mind whether she wanted to or not, Simon had made a cloud balloon and attached a basket to it. In a moment they were both inside and floating swiftly down towards the garden.

Simon kept looking through his binoculars.

'He's hitting him again!' he shouted crossly. 'He's a nasty, beastly—'

'You said all that before,' said Katie.

'I'll stop him,' said Simon fiercely. 'If you can make all kinds of things from clouds then I'm sure I should be able to make a catapult.'

And he did.

It took him just a minute to shape a very big catapult. He was delighted to find that there were some springy, stretchy bits. What he did not know was that the Cloud had known what he was thinking and had very wisely put the stretchy bits there for him. He used them for the elastic bits that you pull back. Katie shaped lots of cloud balls about the size of tennis balls.

They were right over the garden now.

And Simon began to fire away.

'Oh, ow! Help! Stop it! It's hailstorming. Ugh, ow, oh, my goodness, ooooh!'

The man who had been hitting the dog ran inside his cottage as fast as he could, trying to shield himself from the rain of bouncy cloud balls that went bonk, clonk, ponk, nonk on his head.

A few seconds later Simon and Katie landed in the garden.

The dog was so pleased to see them. He was evidently quite sure they had come to rescue him. He took one great leap and jumped into the cloud basket with them.

The unkind man was inside the cottage, trying to explain to his wife how it could be hailing while the sun shone on a summer evening. Then they both looked out of the window and were very frightened to see the cloud balloon.

'Don't ever be cruel to animals again,' shouted Simon, as he and Katie blew into the parachute and they began to float upwards.

'We're going to look after your dog now,' shouted Katie, 'and we shall be very kind to him.'

The man felt very guilty, so he did not try to stop them.

Simon also felt a bit guilty taking someone's dog away. But he said to himself that the dog had decided to jump into the basket of his own free will. They could not have put him out again to live with that cruel man.

So they all sailed up to the Cloud and climbed aboard just as the sun was sinking. They ran across the mushroom plain to their bed in the cosy corner of the mountain.

The dog was really only a big puppy. Imagine anyone wanting to hit a puppy. Now he was full of life and fun. He growled fiercely at bits of cloud and tussled with them, sending up masses of cloud flakes. He barked and yapped for sheer joy at having found a new kind of master and mistress.

The man who had been hitting the dog ran inside his cottage as fast as he could, trying to cover his head from the rain of bouncy cloud-balls that went, clonk, ponk, nonk on his head.

12

Simon and Katie dived into their cloud bed, and Simon made a smaller cloud blanket to cover up the dog.

'What are we going to call him?' asked Katie sleepily.

'Rabbits,' said Simon.

'That's no good. There aren't any rabbits on clouds. I vote we call him Rover.'

'If he does much roving, he'll fall off the edge,' said Simon.

'I vote for Timothy, then,' said Katie.

'I know,' said Simon: 'Timothy Tumbles, because he's always falling about in the clouds.'

That is how their dog came to have such a funny name.

Now they were three adventurers. The Cloud Children and their dog. On their very first day they had done one good deed.

They all fell into a deep, warm sleep, wondering what other adventures lay in store for them. And all through the night the Big Cloud drifted slowly and quietly across the skies.

If you had been awake that night and looking up at it in the moonlight, you might almost have said that the Cloud was smiling.

Chapter 3

SIMON ON THE CLOUD LILO

———

Katie woke up the next morning to find her face all warm with sunshine, and a little bit of the cloud blanket tickling her nose.

Simon and the dog were nowhere to be seen. Then she saw them. They were striding back from the mountain like astronauts on the moon. At least Simon was. Timothy Tumbles was rolling and bouncing his way down like a furry football.

Simon brought three bowls full of cornflakes that he had scrunched up from the most golden sunny part of the Cloud. Also, he had with him some creamy white balls of cloud. When he squeezed them, they turned into milk. It seemed that the Cloud was still being as magic as ever.

'I just couldn't find any dog biscuits,' said Simon. 'So Timothy Tumbles had to have cornflakes too.'

Katie imagined – just imagined, of course – that the Cloud heaved a big sigh when it heard Simon mention dog biscuits. From somewhere right inside the Cloud she thought she heard a rumbly voice which murmured, 'Very sorry.'

She herself felt sorry for the Cloud, which was looking after them very well, but Simon did not appear to hear anything, so she did not mention it. Girls are more sensitive about a cloud's feelings than boys. She supposed the Cloud had not really been expecting to have a dog to feed as well as children.

Simon suddenly shot up into the air, upsetting what was left of his cornflakes.

'He was right,' he shouted.

'Who was right?' asked Katie.

'Sam,' said Simon. 'He said that time stood still when you got onto the Cloud. My watch still says four o'clock yesterday, which was the twentieth. And that was the time we sailed up to the Cloud.' He laughed. 'Mummy won't even have called us for tea yesterday.'

Simon had a watch that gave the date as well as telling the time. Katie did not know why boys always got so excited about uninteresting things like times and dates and watches and suchlike. She decided that when they got home she would ask Daddy to buy her a watch like Simon's, and maybe then she could work it out.

She had a roll about in the clouds with Timothy Tumbles. That was great fun.

Some beautiful butterflies chased each other in and out of the cloud banks. Simon said they were red admirals, but then Simon said all coloured butterflies were red admirals, so Katie was not sure.

Katie wished she could fly like them. Maybe she would try it one day. Maybe she could find a magic way.

Soon the sun was shining brightly. The sky was blue. The Cloud was sailing along like a great ship, and down below they could already see the English Channel.

Simon leaned over the edge. Katie caught hold of his leg and Timothy Tumbles grabbed the sole of his shoe with his teeth, to make sure he did not fall.

But Simon was too eager to see everything. And, of course, what do you think happened? He fell off the edge.

'Oh, sausages!' shouted Katie.

There was her brother hurtling like a stone towards Brighton beach, which was immediately below them. He would land with a terrible bump and Katie could hardly bear to look at him.

But the Cloud, as usual, was looking after them.

'This is Cloud speaking,' it said. 'Cloud to Simon. Cloud to Simon. Are you receiving me? Over.'

Simon was almost too astonished to reply. But then, as the ground continued to rush up at him, he said quickly, 'Simon to Cloud. Simon to Cloud. I hear you. I hear you. Please tell me what to do. Over.'

The voice came again: 'Cloud to Simon. There's a cloudlet underneath you. Just spread yourself out on it. Lie back and think hard that you are as light as a feather.'

'Simon to Cloud. Very good, sir. I will, if I can,' said Simon in a shaky voice.

But he kept looking down and saw Brighton beach and the pier rushing up at him as fast as an express train.

'Don't look down,' boomed the Cloud. 'That will make you feel afraid. Just lie back. Have confidence in the cloudlet. It's there to save you. The cloudlet will bring you back.'

And a very tiny voice, just like that which you might imagine a cloudlet might have, said from beneath him, 'Yes, lie back, Simon. I'll take you back.'

So Simon did. He lay back on the cloudlet just as Daddy had taught him how to lie back in the sea and float.

Slowly but surely, he felt the cloudlet underneath him swell out and hold him up, so that in a moment or two he was not falling at all; he was floating along. It was like being on a lilo made of cloud.

Looking up, he could see Katie and Timothy Tumbles looking down anxiously at him from the edge of the Big Cloud.

When he gained more confidence, he had a quick look down. Hundreds of people on the beach were running about and shouting and pointing at him.

Well, after all, it is not often that a boy drops off a cloud and starts falling on top of your deckchairs just as you are having your morning ice cream.

The lilo cloud was very comfortable. Simon felt he could have stayed there all day. It was lovely and warm. He and the little cloud floated along below the Big Cloud rather like a baby fish swims alongside its mother in the sea.

All the crowd below were gasping. They had never seen anything so remarkable. Some of them were saying the children must be from outer space.

PC Kindly, who was on duty on the front at Brighton that morning, thought at first he had better ring up the fire station to see if they had a ladder long enough to rescue the boy. But he looked so comfortable that PC Kindly sat down on a deckchair to watch for a while. It was easier that way, he thought, to look up at the sky.

Simon became rather bold and kneeled up to get a look at the people down below. After nearly falling off again, he suddenly remembered they were supposed to do helpful things. So he formed a little telescope out of a bit of the cloudlet and looked around the beach. It was as if he were standing on the beach next to people.

Then he froze.

Through the telescope he saw a small hand creep up over the top of a deckchair and unhook a handbag that belonged to an old lady who was sunning herself. Then a young boy in a blue shirt and grubby white shorts stole away, holding the handbag under his shirt. It all happened without PC Kindly seeing anything.

Simon did not know what to do. He could not get down to the beach to stop the boy. Could he make use of the magic cloud tube?

Yes, of course he could. That is just what magic cloud tubes are for. You only have to use your imagination, and you can do all kinds of marvellous things with clouds.

So, instead of listening through it as he had done when they had passed Sam's house, he put his lips to the end of the tube and spoke through it. But he did not speak in his normal voice – which is just as well, because speaking ordinarily through magic cloud tubes makes your voice sound like a roar.

Instead he pointed it straight at the boy who had stolen the handbag and whispered, 'I've seen you take the handbag. You are very naughty. But if you take it back to the lady and apologise, I won't tell the policeman.'

It was as if the young thief had been struck to stone in his tracks. He looked up, down, back, all around and then finally at the mysterious cloud. Then he began to shake with fear that he might be arrested.

'I'll never steal anything again,' he said. 'I promise, I promise, I promise.'

And he took the bag back to the lady and confessed.

He pointed it straight at the boy who had stolen the handbag and whispered.
"I've seen you take the handbag. You are very naughty."

Simon whispered to PC Kindly what he had done, and PC Kindly – who did not have a name like that for nothing – nodded in agreement.

The old lady was very cross with the boy, but she let him go, and he was so frightened by the whole business that he never stole anything more in his whole life.

Katie, who was watching and listening, thought, *Simon is really a very kind boy*. She was proud of her brother.

Simon floated back upwards.

PC Kindly had dozed off in the deckchair for a moment, because it was so nice and warm. He was dreaming that he was a very young boy riding on the clouds through the blue sky.

Chapter 4

SAVING THE MOUNTAINEERS

When Simon came aboard the Big Cloud again, Katie said to him crossly, 'Just don't ever do that again, Simon. You gave me and Timothy Tumbles the frights of our lives.'

She had forgotten that a moment before she had felt very proud of him.

'Oh, I'm all right,' said Simon, and he gave both his sister and Timothy Tumbles a big hug. Katie was quite surprised. She did not usually get hugs from Simon. Actually, he was rather glad to be back.

'The Cloud looked after me,' said Simon, importantly. 'It talked to me.'

'Oh, that's nothing,' replied Katie. 'It talked to me before breakfast this morning – long before it talked to you.'

So there you are. When there are brothers and sisters, neither side can ever win.

The Cloud had now begun to speed up and zoom across the English Channel. They could see many ships down below.

'I'm jolly hungry,' said Katie.

'That's nothing new,' said Simon rudely.

So Katie chased him in gigantic strides across the cloud mushroom plain that led to the foot of the mountain.

On the way Katie fell over and knocked against one of the mushroom-shaped cloud tops.

The mushroom lid fell off.

Inside was the most wonderful collection of cloud ice cream you could imagine. They had found the cloud ice-cream freezer, full of fluffy, chunky, cold ice cream.

Simon made some cloud plates and then collected some vanilla and cream, strawberry ripple, walnut whirl, and pink, white and brown Neapolitan ice creams, all mixed up, with some peppermint ice on top.

Simon and Katie made little cloud spoons and sat on a bank in the sunshine and ate until they thought they would very probably burst. Timothy Tumbles had some – but he did not need a spoon.

'Well,' said Simon, 'we have managed to do two good things, haven't we?' He patted Timothy Tumbles on the head. Saving Timothy had been a good turn for all of them.

I wonder what the next adventure will be, Simon thought.

Little did he know what a desperate test of courage they were all to face.

But for the moment all was warm and safe. They felt full and rather sleepy. The Cloud sailed on over the fields of France.

That afternoon they climbed all the way to the topmost peaks of the Cloud. It was great fun because if you fell off one, you simply landed on a great white springy cloud mattress down below and bounced up again.

Of course, this does not apply to all clouds – to the grey, rainy ones, for instance. You would not bounce on those. You would go straight through and hit the ground with a tremendous bonk. The only clouds where you can bounce and spring about are the great and magic clouds that carry the Cloud Children.

Timothy Tumbles took to diving off one cloud peak and bouncing over to another. Simon did it too, but, as he landed upside down and got his mouth full of cloud, he was a bit more careful next time. Katie expected it was the Cloud's way of telling him not to be too clever.

When they were coming down, they all stopped and began sniffing the beautiful smell that was coming from somewhere.

They soon found it. And it turned out to be just what they had suspected. Do you know what it could have been?

Yes, beans.

They had come across a rosy bank of cloud that had a

wonderful store cabinet filled with beans in tomato sauce. They put slices of cloud bread that they were able to cut from a cliff nearby (it had that beautiful new bread smell) into a toaster that Sam had shown them. Then they put large helpings of beans onto the toast.

In next to no time they were eating beans on toast. On a cloud, half a mile above France.

Some people might have thought that was just not possible. But, then, most grown-ups forget the remarkable things that can happen to children. They forget the wonderful things that happened to them when they were children.

As the Cloud was sailing over the beautiful city of Paris, the wind seemed to spring up from nowhere. It was the beginning of a very big adventure. Simon could have had no idea how big it was going to be.

The wind was from the north, so they were quite cold. They hurried down the mountain and tucked themselves into their cosy cloud bed.

The wind became stronger and stronger and they began to race through the air as if the Cloud had turned into a jumbo jet. They zoomed over France and were over Switzerland in next to no time.

After a while the sky became very black, even though it was still daylight. Rumbles of thunder came from the distance and there were flashes of lightning. Katie and Timothy Tumbles both put their heads under the blanket.

The wind got wilder and wilder and the Cloud was tossed about like a ship in a rough sea.

Even though they were rushing along they could see that they were now right in among the mountains. Swiss mountain tops zipped past them on all sides. Then Simon, who had poked his nose round the corner of the cloud mountain, let out a shriek.

Racing towards them out of the darkness was the sheer, white, snow-covered cliff of an enormous mountain.

They were heading straight for it.

'We're going to crash,' he yelled. 'Get ready for the biggest bump you've ever—'

But no bump came. The Cloud hit the mountain, all right: one of the biggest and most dangerous peaks for climbers in the world. But there was no bump.

The Cloud – for it was a very clever and experienced cloud – just wrapped itself around the mountain like a huge blanket. And hung on.

So, there were Simon and Katie and Timothy Tumbles sitting – fortunately, tucked up tightly in bed – on the side of a cloud mountain, which was wrapped around a real mountain.

Silence – except for the wild wind.

And then – in the wind – they heard cries.

Voices were shouting out, 'Help, help, help!' They sounded desperate.

'W-what are you going to do?' Katie asked fearfully.

Simon was an intelligent and quick-witted young man. He knew that the Cloud would not have wrapped itself around the mountain for no reason at all.

It was quite clear. The reason was that the Cloud was trying to rescue whoever was shouting for help. And the Cloud needed Simon's help to do that.

He summoned up all his courage.

He quickly wrapped himself in a cloud coat and made a cloud cap, cloud earmuffs, cloud gloves and cloud shoes. Now he would not freeze to death.

The wind nearly blew him away, but he had taken the precaution of making a great coil of cloud rope. He tied one end around a cloud boulder, hung on to the other part and then ventured to the edge.

What he saw made him feel sick and dizzy.

Fifty feet below him, huddled on the icy face of the mountain, were three climbers whose rope had broken and who were hanging on for their lives.

It really did look a terrible situation. All three were frozen over in icicles. They looked more dead than alive. Every second their grip on the ledge was loosening.

Simon only had a matter of moments in which to act to save their lives.

He began to work like mad. He tied the loose end of the Cloud rope around himself and then began to lower himself hand over hand off the edge of the Cloud.

Down, down, down.

The wind buffeted him against the icy mountain, but fortunately his cloud coat kept him from getting hurt – and from freezing.

The cries of the men were becoming fainter and fainter. They were at the end of their strength.

When Simon got to them, they were beginning to lose their grip on the edge. They would have fallen thousands of feet.

When they saw Simon, their eyes lit up in their frozen faces. To them it was a miracle.

Simon very much hoped that the Cloud would allow the men to use the cloud rope. Usually grown-ups are far too heavy to walk even on one of the Big Clouds or to use cloud ropes.

But, of course, the Cloud understood. It was the men's cries that had caused the Cloud to wrap itself around the mountain and try to save them.

Through the wind, Simon heard, 'Cloud to Simon. Cloud to Simon. Get the men to come up the cloud rope. Over.'

Simon responded, 'Wilco. Out.'

First, Simon and one of the men, who was not too exhausted, climbed back up the cloud rope. It held all right.

Then the leader of the team, who had stayed on the ledge, tied his other companion in a kind of sling, and Simon and the first man pulled him up.

It all sounds very simple to put it on paper. But there were times when Simon felt sure they could not succeed. The Cloud itself was struggling to hang on to the mountain. The winds screeched. The cold was terrible. The men were exhausted.

When he got to them, they were beginning to lose their grip of the edge.
They would have fallen thousands of feet.

But with a great effort they managed to haul up the poor man, who had been so weak he had nearly slipped off the edge. Then they lowered the rope again and pulled up the leader, who had waited until last to be saved.

All the men collapsed onto the soft cloud. Katie, who was now also wrapped in a cloud coat, covered them with layers of cloud blankets and they were soon asleep.

All that night Simon and Katie and Timothy Tumbles watched over the men.

In the morning, the wind had dropped, it was warmer, and when the men woke it seemed they had had a very refreshing sleep. Katie herself had noticed how nice it was sleeping on the Cloud. Every time you went to sleep you woke up feeling ever so much better. Not tired at all.

'We thank you from the bottom of our hearts,' said the leader in halting English. Simon thought they were from Germany. 'If it had not been for your brave rescue we should all have fallen from the mountain and been killed,' he went on.

Simon felt very proud of himself. Katie felt very proud of Simon. Timothy Tumbles felt proud of both Simon and Katie. And they all felt very grateful to the Cloud and very thankful that it was so clever and strong.

The men were very hungry, so Simon went off at once to the strong beef soup part of the Cloud that he had discovered. He heated up helpings for everyone by putting cloud bowls full of it in the ovens.

Soon the men were feeling much stronger. They gave Simon and Katie some of their badges and a flag they had hoped to put on top of the mountain.

The storm had passed, and the sun was shining. The Cloud – which seemed to be purring a little – let go of the mountain and floated down over a lovely Swiss valley.

The Cloud stopped over a little town whose houses had sharply sloping roofs with snow on them. The climbers found themselves standing opposite the balcony of their hotel. They stepped off the Cloud.

'Goodbye, and thank you again for your brave rescue,' they shouted as the Cloud began to rise into the sunshine.

Katie looked over at Simon. 'I think you were very brave.'

She was surprised to find how modest Simon was.

'I'll tell you what,' he said: 'I think the Cloud was.'

And they both heard the purring noise from the middle of the Cloud turn into a positive hum of pleasure.

Chapter 5

THE DISAPPEARING STAIRCASE

Soon they found themselves floating over the Mediterranean Sea. Blue as blue could be. It was here that they found themselves in a lot of trouble through Simon being too adventurous. They were only saved by – you will never guess who.

A French boy and girl.

You know how a jet plane, when it climbs high into the sky, leaves behind it a trail of white cloud? And, sometimes, when the sun shines on it, the long thin trail of cloud turns silver or golden? That is what Simon saw one day as they floated along.

A jet plane came zooming up and passed quite close to the Big Cloud. The pilot waved and smiled. All the world's airline pilots know about the Secret Army of the Cloud Children, so they always go around the Big Clouds.

The plane left behind it a wonderful cloud staircase, its steps turned into gold by the morning sun.

'Come on,' cried Simon. 'I'm going to climb up the golden ladder to the sky.'

'You'd better not,' said Katie. 'You might fall off. Or there might be a step missing and you would fall through the hole.'

'Oh, don't be a misery,' said Simon crossly. 'Of course we won't fall through a hole.'

In the end he persuaded Katie to come with him, but he could scarcely have imagined how right she was.

Timothy Tumbles decided to stay at home and bark at them.

Simon and Katie jumped onto the cloud steps and began to run up them. Simon said he could see some beautiful salmon-pink cloud high above them and they could have a rest there before they came down again.

Katie was not at all sure. She liked butterflies, but not the kind you get in your tummy when you feel frightened. And those were what she had now.

At first it was very exciting. It was like running up the secret steps to some wonderful temple. Up and up and up they ran, until poor Katie was completely out of breath. So they stopped for a moment.

Katie thought she could hear the Big Cloud grumbling away to itself far below them. Perhaps they were not supposed to do this kind of thing.

When she looked down it seemed a long way back. But when she looked up it seemed even further – much further – to the top.

Another thing. The steps they had come up looked to her as if they were getting thinner. Or, to put it another way, there was not as much of them there as there had been when the children had run up them.

She pulled at Simon's sleeve.

'Yes, what is it?' he asked, in a very stern voice. He was looking out over the vast blue sea and sky and imagining he was the ruler of the world.

'The steps are disappearing,' Katie said.

'Don't disturb his majesty just now,' began Simon, and then, 'What? What did you say?'

'The steps are disappearing behind us,' repeated Katie. She pointed.

There was no doubt about it. All the steps behind them were getting very thin and flaky. The ones up ahead were all right still. But the ones below definitely had a 'drop through' look about them.

What Simon had forgotten, of course, was that the vapour cloud made by aircraft when they fly high into the sky evaporates – that is, disappears into the air again – quite quickly after the aeroplane has passed by. You have a look at the aircraft trails in the sky next

"The steps are disappearing behind us," repeated Katie. She pointed. There was no doubt about it. All the steps behind them were getting very thin and flaky.

time you see them. They are very white and cotton-wool-looking behind the plane. Further back, they drop away into big blobs, and then disappear altogether.

Down below them the Big Cloud seemed to be shaking all over with worry. Timothy Tumbles was barking himself hoarse.

'What are we going to do?' asked Katie.

'We'll, we'll, er, just have to go on up a bit,' said Simon, trying to sound calm, 'and try to make a cloud parachute or something.' He really was not too sure.

And that is what they did. They rushed up the steps until they could not rush any more. In the end, it was a matter of trying to keep just in front of the steps that were disappearing.

But when they stopped, panting, they saw that nearly all the steps behind had gone. And even the ones in front were looking pretty wobbly.

'Try a parachute,' yelled Katie.

Simon grabbed an armful of thin cloud and blew into it. But, of course, clouds made by aeroplanes are not at all the same as pieces from the Big Clouds. Simon's breath just blew a wispy hole.

'Oh, crumbs,' he gasped, 'we're done for.'

They were thousands of feet above their Cloud, on a staircase that was disappearing beneath their feet.

It was certainly a terrible situation. Katie wondered if they should pluck up the courage to jump off the steps without parachutes and hope to have a soft bouncy landing on the Big Cloud. But then she realised that they would probably bounce up again so high they would go over the edge and fall all the way down to the sea.

They had been very thoughtless, but the Big Cloud had realised what kind of danger they were getting themselves into. Whilst they had been running up the cloud steps, the Big Cloud had been sending out an SOS: a distress signal.

'Cloud 82 calling. Cloud 82 calling. Am over middle of Mediterranean. Urgently need help to rescue two children. Any Big Clouds in this area please proceed in this direction at once.'

That was the message that the Cloud had sent out.

By great good fortune, Cloud 99 (there were a hundred of them altogether, so watch out for them) was floating not far from them over the northeast coast of Africa.

Within a matter of minutes Cloud 99 had hurried over and suddenly came up alongside Simon and Katie, who were practically standing on thin air. In another moment they would have been on their way down, fast.

As the other Big Cloud – No. 99 – drew alongside, Simon and Katie were amazed to see the smiling faces of two children peering over the side at them. They were, in fact, French. It was a French brother and sister.

'Don't worry, we will soon rescue you.' said the French boy in what was really very good English. At any rate, it was a great deal better than Simon or Katie's French.

Dropping a cloud rope over the side, the French boy and his sister had Katie and Simon aboard in a moment.

Not a second before time. When Katie looked back to where they had been standing, there was nothing there – just empty sky.

'Thank you very much indeed,' said Simon. He struggled with himself for a moment, wondering whether to admit he had been wrong.

He decided to blame the clouds.

'It would have been all right if the steps had stayed put,' he said.

The French children, who said their names were Pierre and Sophie, smiled.

'Better stay on the Big Cloud and not try to balance on the sky,' said Pierre.

They all laughed, and Simon said, 'Well, it was my fault, really. I shall have to take care of my sister better, won't I?'

Katie was surprised he had said that. But she liked it.

'Anyway,' said Simon to Pierre and Sophie, 'you certainly saved our bacon.'

'Very sorry,' replied Pierre, looking puzzled, 'we don't have bacon on this Cloud.'

Simon tried to explain that 'saving someone's bacon' was an English way of talking about rescuing someone. It was rather hard for the other children to understand, and Sophie said, 'No bacon – but we have lovely roast pork. This Cloud has a whole cave made out of roast pork.'

So they all sat down and had a marvellous meal of roast pork, with cloud potatoes – all chopped up small. Simon and Katie made good friends with Pierre and Sophie.

At last, the two Big Clouds drew close together and it was possible to jump from one to the other. Simon and Katie rolled among their own soft cloud cushions. Timothy Tumbles was overjoyed to see them, but the Big Cloud was rather cross.

They waved and waved until Pierre and Sophie were tiny specks on their cloud. They were very sorry to lose their new friends. They hoped they might see them again one day – perhaps in France.

Chapter 6

THE DAY THE CLOUD SNEEZED

Their next adventure was actually on the Cloud itself. Well, when you come to think of it, there is no better place to find an adventure than on a cloud sailing high in the sky.

It happened like this.

Simon – who was very inquisitive, of course – had found some caves in the cloud mountain. They were quite big and he could walk into them without bending down.

He and Timothy Tumbles went into one of them one day – without telling Katie where they were going.

After they had walked a few yards the tunnel began to slope downhill. They went on, down and down, and the light became greyer and fuzzier. Very cloudy, in fact. It was a bit spooky, and Simon began to wonder – especially after his escape from the cloud staircase – whether they should not go back.

Timothy Tumbles gave a little whimper, rather as if he were in favour of going back.

After a while, Simon realised that all around them there was a buzzing and whirring noise, like the engines of a big ship at sea.

'We'll just have a look round the next corner,' said Simon.

But when he got to the next corner, of course, he said, 'We had better have just a peep round the next corner.'

And so on and so on.

They went across a lot of crossroads, where different tunnels met, so after a while they did not know which way would take them out.

As well as that, the cloud passages kept changing shape. Once, one of them turned right over, or seemed to, and Simon was sure they were walking with their feet – or paws, in the case of Timothy – on the ceiling.

Simon did not know, of course, that one of the funny things about clouds is that, when you are right inside them, it is often impossible to tell their floors from their ceilings.

Just as he was becoming really worried, a deep voice asked, 'What are you doing down here? No brothers, sisters or dogs are allowed down here. This is the SECRET AREA.'

Simon nearly jumped out of his skin, and Timothy Tumbles put his nose in between his front paws.

The voice was very frightening. It sounded like the Cloud's voice. But it was so booming – especially when it spoke of the secret area – that Simon could not be sure. It seemed to come out of the cloud walls themselves.

'I'm very sorry,' quavered Simon. 'We found the caves and wondered where they led to.'

'Well, they lead here, don't they?' said the voice, booming again.

'But – but,' said Simon, 'please – where is here?'

'Oh, what a stupid boy,' said the voice. 'Here is the middle, of course. You're in the very middle of the Cloud.'

'What – what – goes on here?' asked Simon. He felt more than a little frightened, and he realised he had no idea how to get out again.

'What goes on here?' repeated the voice in amazement, as if only a truly ignorant boy could ask a question like that.

'I'm very sorry for being so ignorant, sir,' said Simon. He realised he had better be very polite if he did not want to get into a lot more trouble.

'Well,' said the voice, more kindly, 'I'll forgive you. I'm in rather a bad temper this morning. Some mornings things don't go quite right, do they? Even on a magic cloud. Well, do they?'

'Er – no, sir – yes, sir.' Simon did not quite know which answer to give.

'Well, make your mind up, young man,' said the voice, becoming rather cross again, 'and as to what goes on here, well, I simply cannot tell you, can I? The whole of it is absolutely top-priority, first-class SECRET.'

Every time the voice came to the word *SECRET* it boomed it out so that they were nearly deafened. Simon thought that probably people all over the world could hear it.

'Here are all our secret cloud engines that make us go and stop and rise and fall and rain and turn round and freeze your ice cream and fry your bacon and chips. There, I have told you. So now you know. And it is all absolutely secret. So you must not tell a soul.'

'Are you the person who drives the Cloud?' asked Simon.

'Don't be silly, boy. I am the Cloud,' replied the voice. And it laughed very loudly so that the whole Cloud shook, and in the cave poor Simon and Timothy were nearly deafened. 'There aren't any persons in Cloudland. We are just one cloud working together. It seems to me that the sooner you human beings have the same system – a bit more togetherness and less "I want" – the better you will all get on.'

'Yes, sir,' said Simon.

'There is another reason you shouldn't be down here,' said the cloud. It suddenly sounded a bit wheezy.

'Why is that, sir?'

Simon was still answering very correctly. He felt rather as if he were talking to his headmaster.

'Because – because,' said the Cloud, sniffing and wheezing even more, 'when you come down here through all my tunnels you – you – tickle me – and make me want to … want to … want to …'

'Want to what, sir?' asked Simon.

'Want to sneeze,' shouted the Cloud. 'Atishooooo! Atishooooo! Atishooooo!'

When the voice – which was the Cloud, of course – sneezed, the whole Cloud, and everything in it and on it, shook and quivered and quavered and rolled about and bounced up and down and was thrown in all directions. Simon and Timothy Tumbles rolled around the walls of the cloud cave as if they were marbles.

Poor Katie, up on top, was just having a sunbathe when she found herself flung twenty feet in the air and came down twice to be shot back up again at each *atishooooo*.

Simon and Timothy Tumbles rolled around the walls of the cloud cave as if they were marbles. Poor Katie up on top, was just having a sunbathe when she found herself flung twenty feet in the air...

Arab people watching from a little town in North Africa, over which they were passing, thought the Cloud was going to explode. It rocked and quivered and sent little bits of cloud flying in all directions, not to mention some rain, which pleased the Arabs very much.

Eventually it all settled down and Simon and Timothy sat looking at each other.

'I do beg your pardon,' said the Cloud.

'Granted, sir,' said Simon politely.

The Cloud sounded friendly again and less wheezy. 'Now, off you go, young man – and, er, young dog – up to the top again. We have another adventure coming up for you very soon. And just remember,' it boomed, 'not a word to anyone about the secret things I told you about.'

Then, almost to itself, it added, 'How funny. Whenever I start to talk about secret things, I always want to shout it out and tell everybody. Tut, tut, tut. Very strange. I shall have to be rather cross with myself.'

'Please, sir, how do we get out?' asked Simon.

'Oh, my dear chap,' said the Cloud, sounding much more friendly, 'it's perfectly easy. The rule is this. When you are in a cloud, always keep turning to your right. And you will come out – on this Cloud, anyway – right next to the bacon and chips counter.'

'Ooh, good,' said Simon wistfully. And then, 'Thank you very much, sir.' The mention of bacon and chips had made him think of tea.

'Oh, and by the way,' said the Cloud, 'we've got some dog biscuits on board now. We're sorry we didn't have any the other day. But then, we did not really expect to have a dog on board. Whatever you do, don't bring an elephant on board if you go down to Africa, will you?' And it laughed very heartily, making the Cloud wobble alarmingly once again.

Simon and Timothy Tumbles rushed up the passages, turning right all the time. They heard the Cloud shouting to them, 'The dog biscuits are in a cloud cupboard next to the chips.'

A few moments later they emerged into the wonderful sunshine.

'Gosh,' said Simon, 'I'll bet nobody – not even any other brothers and sisters – has been right down to the middle of their Cloud.'

He gave Timothy some cloud dog biscuits. Then he made some bacon and chips for himself and Katie and went back to tell her all about the secret area in the middle of the Cloud.

How strange. He was like the Cloud. As soon as he started thinking of the secret things he had been told, he wanted to shout them out to everyone else.

Perhaps we are all like that. We just cannot keep secrets. Can we?

Chapter 7

ALI AND THE PIRATES

In the hot days that followed, Katie built a cool cloud house. The house itself was in the shade, but the little terrace was in the sun, and here they could sunbathe.

She moulded some chairs and a table out of cloud so that they could eat their meals more easily. She also made a dog kennel for Timothy Tumbles. She even modelled a telephone out of cloud – just to remind her of her mum's sitting room at home, because she was still a little bit homesick.

Imagine their surprise when one morning the telephone began to ring.

Buzz, buzz, buzz. Zing, zing, zing. It rang quite sharply, commanding them to pick it up.

Simon did so.

'Hello,' he said, hesitantly. He could not think that anyone might be at the other end.

But someone was.

'Ah, good morning,' said the deep voice. 'Cloud here. Very good of your sister to fix up a telephone. Saves using the cloud radio all the time. Never could understand this "over and out" business. Anyway, I just wanted to tell you, young man, that your next adventure is down below. That is, on the sea. Kindly go to the edge and have a look and tell me what help you want.'

Plonk. And the voice had rung off.

'Help,' cried Simon, 'an adventure happening on the sea. We'd better go and have a look. Quick.'

They all rushed to the edge of the Cloud.

They were floating over the sparkling Arabian Sea now, on their way to India. They could see the sandy coastline of Saudi Arabia and the several smaller Arab states there.

But what came immediately into view in Simon's cloud telescope was the drama that was taking place on the deck of a small sailing ship right underneath the Cloud.

A band of rascally-looking men were clustered around a small Arab boy who was tied to the mast with thick ropes. The men, some with beards, had knives and curved swords like cutlasses. One of them had placed the tip of his knife at the throat of the poor boy.

It was obvious they meant to kill him.

'Jiminy cricket, but we've got to be quick,' shouted Simon.

The phone was back at the house, so he had to use the cloud radio.

'Hello, Cloud. Hello, Cloud,' he called. He rather liked doing it this way. 'Come in, Cloud. Over.'

'How can I come in and roll over, or whatever you're asking me to do?' retorted the Cloud crossly, without using the usual signals for radio. 'Just tell me what you want me to do. Now, quickly. Over and out and up and down and round the corner to you too.'

'Sorry, Cloud,' shouted Simon, who could not help laughing a little even though the situation on the ship was desperate. 'Please descend to just over the ship. Also urgently need shield made of the toughest and stickiest cloud you have. And some very sticky cloud cannon balls.'

'Cloud here,' boomed the Cloud. 'Good thinking, Master Simon. I get the plan. There are sticky shields in the sticky shield cupboard – two jumps to your right. Mind you don't get stuck to them. Sticky cannon balls in same cupboard. Sticky on one side only. Mind you pick up by the right side. Sticky side looks very custardy.'

Then the Cloud laughed. 'Ha ha ha. Ho ho ho. I know what you're going to do.' It was evidently very pleased with Simon.

In seconds, Simon had got what he wanted. Firstly, a huge thick round cloud shield, one side of which was as sticky as toffee. And, secondly, a great bag full of very splodgy cloud cannon balls. Fortunately, it was a non-stick cloud bag.

41

The Cloud was going down quickly now. Katie had made a cloud ladder for Simon, and he began to climb down.

'Oh, do be careful,' Katie shouted. She didn't like the look of the sharp swords of the men on the boat at all.

But Simon knew just what he was going to do. That was one of the nice things about being on the Cloud. It seemed to help you make up your mind quickly.

He swung down the ladder and sprang onto the deck of the ship, which was obviously a pirate ship, before any of the men realised what was happening.

They all turned their fierce faces towards him, and he saw the sun gleaming on their knives and cutlasses. He had to admit he felt very frightened of them.

But they did not seem a bit frightened of him, although they looked surprised to see his big shield. They seemed to be about to cut him up into small pieces.

One man rushed at him and aimed a great blow with his sword.

But that was where Simon's shield came in handy.

The villain thought it was just a piece of cloud and that he would slice it in two, and Simon with it. Imagine his surprise when his sword got stuck in the shield. It went in – and stopped. And the man could not pull it out.

That had been Simon's idea, of course, in asking for very sticky cloud.

Another and another of the pirates tried to stab or slice Simon. But each time, Simon put up his shield and the dagger or sword went in and got stuck there. Nothing the men could do could get the weapons out again. After a while, the shield looked like the back of a porcupine with all its spines sticking up.

Then one man raised a pistol and fired some shots at Simon, but he ducked behind the shield. The shots went in, all right. But they did not come through. They had got stuck too.

The men became very excited then and began to rush at Simon with their fists. But he was ready for them.

He grabbed the squelchy cannon balls out of the bag, taking care

He grabbed the squelchy cannon balls out of the bag, taking care not to touch the very sticky, custardy side, and threw them as hard as he could at the men.

not to touch the very sticky, custardy side, and threw them as hard as he could at the men.

The effect was just like you see in old films when people throw custard pies at each other. Each one landed *splosh* on a pirate's face. And once the cloud pies were on their faces they just could not get them off.

They really were in a mess. They could not see. The sticky custard cloud stuck to their faces, their hair, their beards, their hands. They staggered about the deck, heaving away at the custard and all the time becoming more entangled. They all began to look as if they had just struggled out of a pot of glue.

Simon had won the battle. All around him the pirates were rolling about and accidentally sitting on their swords and jumping up again because that hurt.

But that served them right for being so cruel. They had been about to torture the little Arab boy who was tied to the mast.

As Simon was untying him, the boy told Simon his name was Ali Abu. Simon showed Ali the ladder and the little boy climbed up as quickly as he could.

When they got to the Cloud, Ali explained that he lived with his mother, father and siblings in a little fishing village on an island in the Arabian Sea. His father, a fisherman, had been diving to see if there was any treasure in the wreck of an old Portuguese ship sunk hundreds of years ago. The pirates had captured Ali to make him show them where the wreck was.

Ali was very grateful and very impressed with Simon's fighting skill. He was well mannered too. Every so often he would bow to them, holding his hands together in front of his face. Both Simon and Katie liked him very much.

They found it rather hard at first feeding an Arab boy because his food was different. But he quite liked the cornflakes and he thought the ice cream was delicious.

By the end of the day the Cloud had swooped in over the island where Ali lived. Both Katie and Simon had come to like him more and more. He jumped around on the cloud as if he were on springs.

'I've got a sister,' he said. 'I hope the Secret Army of the Clouds will choose us for a trip sometime.'

Katie was sure the Cloud had heard what Ali had said. There was a kind of rumbly noise from below and a clicking as if Ali's name were being put on the computer, or whatever SECRET machine the Cloud kept right down in the SECRET middle area. Perhaps Ali's wish would come true.

They were very sorry to see him go. He climbed down a cloud rope and his mother and father were very pleased to see him. His mother wept because she had thought her son had come to great harm.

While Ali had been on the ship, his father had opened the chests on the sunken wreck and had found they were not full of gold at all. Only musket balls made of lead.

But he didn't seem to mind. A wide grin spread over his brown, wrinkled face. He seemed to be saying, 'We are very happy here being fishermen, even if we are rather poor. When you think you have found money, look what happens. Boatloads of pirates come and steal your son – who is worth more than gold.'

There was no chance of the pirates ever coming back. It took them weeks to get the custardy cloud out of their hair and beards. Their wives would not speak to them. Everyone laughed at them. In the end, they all gave up being pirates.

Ali Abu and his family shouted good wishes to Simon and Katie and Timothy Tumbles as the Big Cloud took off again. Ali and his mother and father and all the family made that nice, friendly sign of putting their hands together in front of their faces and making bows.

Simon and Katie did the same. Although they were sad to leave Ali and certainly hoped they would see him again, they were pleased to see the family so happy.

'Well,' said Simon, as they soared away, 'we have made friends with some French children and some Arab children. Isn't it great? The world isn't as big as I thought. And the different kinds of children in it are not different at all, really. They're all jolly super.'

'They certainly are,' said Katie wistfully. For she had had a bit of a crush on Ali.

Chapter 8

MR UPSIDE-DOWN SINGH

Shortly after that a big wind blew them right over India. The Cloud always sailed on the wind whenever it could. It only used the SECRET cloud engines when it had to alter course and go in a different direction to the wind.

It became very hot indeed, so Katie scooped out a swimming pool and filled it by squeezing water out of some grey, wet bits of cloud.

Of course, clouds – even the Big Clouds – tend to melt away a good bit in hot weather. Once, when Simon was walking along, he came across a great hole in the floor of the Cloud. The hole had not been there before. When he looked down, all he could see were mountains and desert ever so far below.

Riding on clouds is fun, but you have to be very careful sometimes.

Through the telescope they could see a lot of people in tiny, dusty villages. Katie was upset because she saw little Indian children who seemed to have very little to eat.

'I would give them my bacon and chips,' said Simon.

'I wonder why grown-ups from other countries don't send them all some food,' said Katie.

It was a question not even the Cloud could answer.

In one village Simon spotted a terrible thing happening. A very mean man was beating the villagers and farmers with a stick and making them pay him the last few bits of money they had. Those who could not pay he drove out of their homes. Simon and Katie saw several families with lots of thin little children being driven out by this cruel man.

He was the landlord. That is, he owned the land. And he was a wicked one. He made the poor farmers pay him too much just for being allowed to use the land to grow wheat and barley and beans to feed themselves on.

At last the cruel man drove away in a car to his big house nearby. After he had had an enormous meal – enough for four normal people – he rolled into his bed and fell asleep, without even getting changed into his pyjamas. (Katie and Simon washed their clothes every day in cloud soap flakes.) Meanwhile lots of poor families who no longer had any homes were being forced to sleep in the village street.

Simon sat and thought and thought and thought.

'Why don't you do something?' Katie asked him.

'Because I'm thinking what to do, silly,' he said.

'Why don't we take them some cloud food down?' asked Katie. But Simon said that cloud food was not the same when it got to the ground. It was fine for those living on the Cloud, but down below it just turned into rain or fog.

Then, after a little more thinking (during which he had a quiet word or two with the Cloud), Simon shouted, 'I've got it.'

'Oh, good,' the Cloud whispered to Katie. 'I tried to help him make up his mind.'

The Cloud often had a whisper to Katie. She had a nice quiet way of saying, 'Good morning, Cloud,' as if every day was the best day. Whereas every morning Simon shot out of the cloud house, bawled, ''Lo, Cloud,' and promptly fell off a mountain and bounced three hundred feet into the air, or something like that, which was all a bit disconcerting for a cloud who was busy being a cloud and trying to steer round the world.

Anyway, Simon said, 'I've got it.'

And he really had got a good idea.

In the middle of the night he and Katie floated down to earth under a cloud parachute. They landed just outside the big house where they could hear the snores of the cruel landlord. Simon had brought with him some strong cloud strings and two cloud balloons which could be blown up to a great size.

They crept into the house and through into the man's bedroom. They had to be very quiet, and Katie felt rather afraid.

47

'Are you sure we are supposed to come in here?' she asked Simon.

'If you want those poor people to have their homes back, then we have to do something, don't we?' Simon retorted shortly.

The man was heaving up and down in his sleep like a ship at sea.

Very gently Simon tied the cloud strings to the man's two big toes. At the other ends of the pieces of string he fixed the cloud balloons.

It was just beginning to get light when all was ready.

'Now,' said Simon to Katie, 'you blow into one balloon as hard as you can, and I'll blow into the other.'

When Simon had told her they would be big balloons he certainly meant it. Before they were fully blown up, the man was being carried away out of the door.

'Blow harder,' yelled Simon.

They blew and blew and blew, until they had to drop off or they would have gone up with Mr Singh – for that was the landlord's name.

The poor villagers were awake early, for they had had a miserable night. Imagine their amazement as they saw floating slowly over them the hated figure of their cruel landlord. He was tied by his toes to two fat, balloon-like clouds, and was, of course, hanging upside down.

Now, just think what happens when a boy – or a man – stands on his hands or hangs upside down from a tree or a rope.

Why, all the things fall out of his pockets, of course.

Well, all the money that the cruel man had grabbed from the Indian farmers began to fall out of his pockets.

First, his trouser pockets let fall a rain of coins. Then his coat pockets emptied all the bank notes in a fluttering snowfall of money. Every single bit of money came skimming down and landed among the villagers.

Of course, as they believed the man had cheated them for years, they felt the money was theirs anyway. They picked it up. And the families who had been turned out of their houses went back into them.

He was tied by his toes to two fat, balloon like clouds, and was, of course, hanging upside down.

'Thank you, thank you, clouds,' they shouted. 'We shall be able to buy more seed and grain to grow our crops now.'

They all rather hoped that the landlord would fall on his head on top of Mount Everest.

But even if a man is cruel it is wrong to be very cruel to him. The best thing is to try to teach him a lesson and persuade him to be better. There was no doubt that being hung upside down under two clouds and being afraid of dropping all that way on his head was teaching Mr Singh a very sharp lesson indeed.

Simon and Katie sailed back up to the Cloud, which then went alongside Mr Singh.

'Oh, have mercy on me,' Mr Singh kept crying.

Simon said sternly, 'Will you promise never to take money from the villagers again?'

'Oh, I will, I will, I will,' cried Mr Upside-Down Singh.

'Will you promise to use all your money to help the villagers grow their crops and feed their children well?' asked Katie.

'Oh, I certainly will. I do most sincerely promise,' wailed Mr Singh, wrong way up.

'And never hit anyone again?'

'Never, never, never,' cried Mr Upside-Down.

'The Cloud will tell us if you've been telling lies,' said Katie. 'The Cloud is very clever, you know.'

The Cloud rather liked that bit.

'No, he hasn't been telling lies,' said the Cloud in its deep voice. 'I think he has had his lesson now.'

Simon leaned over and poked a cloud stick into the two balloons attached to Mr Singh's toes. That made them lose some air, and Mr Singh began slowly to sink away below them.

Unfortunately, he came down with rather a splosh in a pond in another village.

'Oh, my goodness,' said Mr Singh, squeezing the water out of his clothes, 'I must go and help those poor villagers, or it might all happen to me again.'

He looked up at the Big Cloud, and Simon's voice came down to him through a cloud tube. 'Don't forget, Mr Singh, the Cloud

Children will be keeping an eye on you.'

'Good gracious,' muttered Mr Singh. 'They're going to be watching me every minute. I really must do better. I have been a very bad and cruel man.'

And he hurried away towards his new life.

Happy to say – because there is a lot of good in the worst of us – Mr Singh kept his promise, and the village of which he was the landlord became one of the happiest in India. All the children are well fed, and Mr Singh has built a new school and hospital and library.

And, in the end, all the villagers have come to like him very much.

Chapter 9

'HOP ABOARD,' SAID KATIE TO THE KANGAROO

Simon and Katie sailed on over Malaysia and Indonesia and down the coast of Australia. Below them they could see the Great Barrier Reef, with beautifully coloured fish in the sea. And great sharks too, swimming along with their wicked-looking fins sticking out of the water.

'Ooh, I'm glad I'm not going for a swim down there,' said Simon, as he dived into their cloud swimming pool and splashed about. This was a super way to keep cool.

One day they found themselves floating over the city of Melbourne, and there they had an adventure that Katie thought was very boring and Simon thought was very exciting.

Down below they could see some white dots running about on a green patch of grass.

'It's cricket,' bawled Simon in excitement. 'England are playing Australia.'

Katie's heart sank.

'That old game,' she said crossly. 'I can't imagine anything as dull and boring as cricket.'

'What?' said Simon, amazed that someone could actually dislike cricket. 'It's very exciting. Especially when the batsman hits a six. A six is the biggest hit anyone can make.'

'How boring,' said Katie.

But just at that moment the batsman down on the patch of green below did hit a six.

It was the most terrific and tremendous hit. The ball flew off his bat and went up and up and up into the air, higher than the Cloud on which Simon and Katie were travelling.

'Crikey,' shouted Simon. 'It'll go right through the top of the sky. I wonder if it's going to come down again and if I shall be able to catch it.'

And he began running and leaping from cloud-top to cloud-top, trying to find the right spot to be underneath the ball when it came down.

The ball went up a bit higher and then decided it was probably about time it started to come down again. But it had reckoned without Simon, one of the best bowlers and catchers in the school team.

As the ball came down, Simon held out his cupped hands, and the ball (much to its surprise, and Simon's) fell right in.

It made Simon's hands sting like mad. So much so that he almost dropped it.

'Got it,' he yelled.

'How boring,' murmured Katie.

Simon wondered what he should do.

He realised that, as he was not playing for either side, he could not have caught the batsman out. Indeed, when he looked down, he saw that the umpire had signalled that the hit was, indeed, a six. The teams had gone off for their lunch, assuming that the ball had been hit out of the ground and had been lost.

'Silly old game,' said Katie.

But Simon only smiled. He put the ball on a little fluff of cloud, tied a note to it and sent it gently sailing down to land in the middle of the pitch.

When the players came onto the pitch again, this is what they read:

Here is the ball you lost. A very famous cricketer called Simon caught it. He hopes you remember and then, perhaps, he can play for England one day.
Simon.
P.S. I am on the Cloud.

All the cricketers were amazed. They had never come across anything like this.

They looked up at the Cloud for a long time. One or two thought they could see a boy waving at them, but they could not be sure.

The English captain picked the note up and put it in his pocket. 'I'd better keep this,' he said. 'If Simon caught that ball, on a cloud or on a mountain, he could play for England one day.'

Simon, listening through his cloud tube, jumped up and down for joy.

'Silly old game,' said Katie for the umpteenth time.

Then they sailed right across the middle of Australia, much of which is a terribly hot desert.

One day Katie spotted three people down below. They looked worn out. They huddled together in a bit of shade afforded by their tent. It was obvious at once that they had run completely out of water.

Simon at once picked up the cloud telephone. 'Mr Cloud, sir,' he said, very politely, 'I wonder if you could rain a bit.'

'Whatever next?' exclaimed the Cloud. 'Do you think I can just rain whenever I want to? You will get me into all kinds of trouble if I go raining where I'm not supposed to.'

'But those people down below are dying of thirst,' said Simon.

'Well, they ought to be much more careful,' said the Cloud.

'But saying that doesn't get them any water,' said Simon bravely.

'Oh, all right,' grumbled the Cloud. It knew Simon was right, of course. It was just that it had been having a rather nice sleep and it didn't much want to rain at the moment. It was too hot. 'I'll give them a good pelting for half an hour.'

And it did.

The land surveyors, for that is what they were, thought they had been caught in a flood and could not believe their luck. Often it does not rain in the Australian desert for years at a time.

When the downpour was over the three men were wet through both inside and out and had filled their water bottles for the rest of the journey. They waved gratefully to the Cloud, who was rather pleased with them for doing that.

It said to Simon, 'Good idea of mine, that, to send them some rain down and quench their thirst.' Then it chuckled.

Simon thought the Cloud must be teasing him. And he was right.

At one time, when the Cloud had decided to sail near to the ground (to make a change from sailing high up), Katie saw some kangaroos. They were leaping along with great bounds. Some of the mothers had baby kangaroos peeping out of the pouches which were attached to the mothers' tummies. The babies are called joeys and they looked very cuddly.

'Oh, I would love to have one up here,' said Katie.

'No, certainly not. We can't have that,' boomed the Cloud. 'We had a kangaroo up here once before. He jumped enough on the ground, but when he got up here it was as if he were made of elastic. He bounced hundreds of feet high. Then he fell off.'

'Oh, how terrible,' said Katie.

'He landed in a lake,' said the Cloud, 'and swam out. So he was all right.'

The Cloud was now so low that they were moving practically alongside the group of kangaroos, who seemed to be racing with it.

The Cloud must still have been rather sleepy, or it would have seen what was sure to happen.

Katie just could not resist it. She leaned over the side and shouted to one of the mother kangaroos who had a joey in her pouch, 'Hop aboard. Have a ride on our Cloud.'

The kangaroo gave a big leap and just for a second was on the cloud next to Katie. The joey's little face peeped out of the pouch. He looked very surprised.

But the kangaroo was not standing beside Katie for more than a second. The cloud was very wise, and it had been right. Bouncy clouds are not good places for kangaroos, who are bouncy enough as it is on the ground.

The kangaroo landed, sank several feet into the Cloud and then shot high into the air, only to land on more springy cloud and be catapulted even higher.

The Cloud was now so low that they were moving practically alongside the group of kangaroos who seemed to be racing with it.

Up and down, up and down. Higher and higher. Before long she was going to fall off the Cloud altogether.

Katie felt terrible. If only she had listened to the Cloud. Now the animal and her lovely baby might be hurt, and it would be all her fault.

Then she remembered what the cloud had said about the previous jumping kangaroo who had landed in a lake.

She rushed across to the swimming pool she and Simon had made. It was quite deep, because they could both swim. She waved madly at the kangaroo and pointed to the pool. 'Land in here,' she yelled. 'Land in here.'

It was just as if the kangaroo understood every word. Splosh. On the next graceful downward bound she and her baby landed right in the middle of the pool, and that stopped them bouncing.

'Oh, you don't know how grateful I am, miss,' she said in kangaroo language.

'Me too,' said a squeaky little voice from the depths of the pouch.

Simon and Katie tied mother and baby to a cloud parachute and watched them float gently down to earth again.

That evening the Cloud telephoned the children and said, 'You're doing very well in helping people. I'm very pleased with you.'

'And we're doing well in adventures,' said Simon, thinking of how he had caught the cricket ball.

'And kangaroos,' said Katie.

'Ahem,' said the Cloud sternly, 'I'm not too pleased about that, Miss Katie.'

Nor was Timothy Tumbles. He had been looking sad ever since he had seen how much Katie liked the kangaroo and her baby.

'I can't do anything right, can I?' said Katie. 'Anyway,' she added, noticing Timothy's sad face, 'I like dogs much the best.'

'Good,' said the Cloud.

'Good,' said Timothy Tumbles to himself, looking very happy.

Chapter 10

SIMON TURNS INTO AN ICICLE

Brrr. Brrr. Shiver. Shiver.

It was getting colder and colder. The Big Cloud had carried them away from the heat of Australia, down across the sea towards the South Pole.

They flew for days and days without seeing anything but the great Southern Ocean. It is the most feared by all sailors. It has worse storms than anywhere in the world.

Finally, they came to the ice and snow of the South Pole. If Father Christmas does live there, he must have very good central heating. If he did not, even his whiskers would freeze.

Simon and Katie kept well wrapped up in their cloud coats and put on two extra cloud blankets at night. They even made a special coat for Timothy, with just his tail and his nose sticking out – one at one end and the other at the other end.

When they were over what seemed the worst possible place in the world, with blizzards blowing the snow into huge snowdrifts, Simon suddenly shouted, 'There's someone down there and it looks as if they need help.'

'Cloud to Simon. Cloud to Simon,' said the Cloud, rather sternly (showing that it really knew how to use the radio perfectly well). 'No one at the South Pole is listed by the cloud computer as being in need of help. Proceeding on course. Over and out.'

'Simon to Cloud,' replied Simon. 'I think your computer's gone barmy. Out.'

'How dare you speak to me like that, young man?' said the Cloud, extremely crossly (and forgetting all about the radio bits).

'If a computer says something, we all know that must be right.'

But, just this once, at any rate, the computer was only half right. And Simon was the other half right.

'Look now,' he cried, 'you can just see through the snow that there is a big red cross made from lanterns on the ground.'

The cloud sighed. It had to admit that that was so.

'I'm going down,' shouted Simon, 'to find out if there's anyone hurt. Red lights may mean that there's been an accident.'

'Oh no, you mustn't,' said Katie. She knew it would be dangerously cold out of the protection of their cloud coverings.

'I'll put my cloud coat and gloves and scarf and boots and cap on,' said Simon.

'And earmuffs,' added Katie.

'And earmuffs,' added Simon.

But the Cloud suddenly became very excited. 'They won't keep you as warm down there as they do up here, Master Simon,' it said anxiously. 'Up here they're fine, and even down there they would be okay at quite low temperatures – like on the mountain in Switzerland.'

It was the first time Katie had heard the Cloud excited enough to use a word like 'okay'.

The Cloud went on, 'Down there, the temperatures are perhaps fifty or sixty degrees below zero. That means that your cloud clothes will freeze solid. You'll turn into an icicle.'

'Oh, don't be an old silly,' laughed Simon. 'We've had tougher adventures than this.'

And before the Cloud could respond to this cheeky remark, Simon had gone over the side and down a rope into the swirling snow.

But, oh, help! The Cloud had been right. Before he even reached the ground, everything had frozen. Even the rope down which he was climbing. It became so slippery that he shot down the last bit and landed with a bump in a snowdrift.

As he struggled out of the drift, he felt all the cloud clothes turning into ice. He was in the middle of them and he began to feel very numb. He couldn't feel his fingers or his toes.

In the end, he just stood there, unable to move. As the Cloud had said, he was turning into an icicle.

Suddenly, a door was flung open in what Simon had thought was another snowdrift and a man rushed out. He was all muffled up in furs, but underneath the fur hat Simon could just see that he still wore a naval officer's peaked cap.

'What in the name of the giant sea serpent are you doing here?' he roared at Simon.

Simon tried to say something, but, because he was now frozen into the cloud clothes, no words could be heard. All the captain could see was Simon's mouth opening and shutting like that of a fish in a bowl.

'Take him inside, lads, and thaw him out. Quick, before he gets frostbite.'

And half a dozen hefty sailors who had also come from the door in the snowdrift grabbed hold of Simon-the-icicle, rushed him inside a warm hut that was concealed there and began to thaw him out.

After a few minutes, he stood in a pool of water. The captain had shut the door and the hut was very cosy with a glowing stove.

When Simon emerged from his ice armour the sailors fed him hot soup and he felt much better.

'Now, my lad, where in the Dickens did you come from?' asked the captain.

'Er – from the Cloud, sir,' said Simon.

The captain and the sailors roared with laughter.

'You hear that, lads?' roared the captain. 'This young imp says he came off a cloud. More likely a penguin brought him.'

'No, sir,' replied Simon, very correctly, 'it wasn't a penguin. And I wasn't on *a* cloud, sir. I was on *the Cloud*.'

'Great gobbling polar bears,' said the captain in amazement. 'Is anyone else up there?'

'There's my sister, sir. And Timothy Tumbles, our dog.'

'Well, blow me down with a blizzard,' said the captain. He had some very funny sayings.

Everyone was laughing except the lieutenant, the captain's

In the end, he just stood there, unable to move. As the Cloud had said, he was turning into an icicle.

second in command. He had a quiet word with the captain, and the captain's face became very serious. Simon watched the captain nodding and saying, 'Well, well. Amazing. I'd never have thought it possible.'

The captain put a lot of trust in what his lieutenant told him, and the lieutenant was one of the few grown-ups privileged to know about the Secret Army of Children who ride on the special clouds. And that was because, when he was a boy, he had been one of the Cloud Children himself.

And so, prompted by the captain, Simon told them the whole story: the rescue of the dog, the rescue of the climbers and of Ali, the help for the Indian village, and all the other adventures.

They were all very quiet when he had finished.

Then the captain said, 'We all think you're a couple of very brave youngsters. You have our respect, lad. It was a fine thing to come down here in this freezing cold because you thought we had trouble.'

He went on to tell Simon that the red lights were landing lights for the aircraft that flew in supplies from a nearby base. The blizzard had only just started, and they had been just about to switch the lights off because the plane would not come today.

Simon thought to himself that the men were much braver than he was, because they had volunteered to live in this freezing land for twelve months and study weather changes: things that could make both flying and sailing much safer.

The men all gave Simon a cheer. Up above, Katie wondered what was going on.

The captain asked Simon, 'Do you know what day it is, my lad – that is, in this part of the world?'

Simon had to admit he did not.

'It's Christmas Day,' said the captain, 'and if you can get your sister and your dog down here pretty quick, we'll give you the best slap-up Christmas dinner you've ever had.'

It was not hard to do that. It was very cold for Katie and Timothy at first, but the sailors soon had them inside and thawed out.

They all had turkey and stuffing and sprouts and roast potatoes. And then the chef came in with his white chef's hat on and served them all plum pudding with custard and cream. There were Christmas crackers too, and everyone wore funny hats and sang songs.

The children stayed the night, and the next morning the blizzard had blown itself out.

The Cloud was hovering just above the hut buried in the snowdrift. It was grumbling about people who went off and ate big dinners and never told the Cloud what they were doing, and wasn't the food good enough on the Cloud?

'How are you going to get back up, then, my lad?' the captain asked Simon.

The sailors dressed the children and Timothy in thick coats, hats and gloves. When they peeped out of the door, they saw two pillows of cloud come floating down. The Cloud was very relieved to see the children (in spite of its grumbling) and had sent its special taxi service to collect them.

Simon, Katie and Timothy Tumbles jumped onto the cloud pillows, which sailed them back up to the Cloud. They waved goodbye to the brave men.

'Good luck,' shouted the captain.

'Good luck,' shouted the lieutenant.

All the men waved and shouted goodbye.

And then, as the Cloud sailed away, the men became mere specks in a great white expanse of snow and ice.

Simon felt very proud to have met them. He decided he did not want to be a cricketer after all. He wanted to be an explorer at the South Pole.

Katie and Timothy knew what they wanted. Their cosy beds. And in they went, just as fast as they could, and snuggled down.

Chapter 11

THE SHANTY TOWN

F rom the frozen wastes of the South Pole the Cloud sped swiftly on towards South America. It swept in over Cape Horn, where the children peered down fearfully at the gales lashing the waves up into mountainous crests. Many ships had been sunk there.

The weather began to be much hotter as they made their way over great prairies and huge forests. But it was over one of the South American countries that the Cloud broke down and wept.

Simon and Katie had never seen the Cloud so upset. When they saw what the Cloud was crying about, they began to weep too.

For a while, beneath them, there had been a wonderful modern city with tall buildings and wide roads. It looked rich and comfortable.

Then, just outside the city, they saw the shanty town. This was where all the terribly poor people who could find no homes in the big city lived.

There are shanty towns of one kind or another outside many big cities, but probably the biggest and poorest shanty towns are in South America. Families from the country and the hills come to the cities to try to find better homes. But the cities are already full and the only place they can live is in the shanty towns, which are built out of old bits of wood and boxes and sheets of tin and corrugated iron. They are higgledy-piggledy towns made up of crooked houses like the crooked man in the nursery rhyme used to live in. But they have no clean water and very little food.

Every time the Cloud went over the shanty towns it burst into tears. And, of course, that meant that down below on the earth it rained.

This time it seemed that the Cloud just could not stop weeping.

And, as you know, when a cloud rains or weeps it becomes smaller and thinner.

Suddenly, to their horror, Simon and Katie found themselves slipping through a hole in the bottom of the Cloud. Fortunately, Simon managed to grab a piece of cloud and they used it as a parachute to float down to earth.

They landed right in the middle of the shanty town. All around them were the crooked little houses that families had built for themselves as their only shelter.

It was still raining, because the Cloud was still crying, and Simon and Katie were soon wet through.

They were suddenly met by a priest who was leading a little family of father, mother and three children. They were all carrying pieces of old wood, sheets of corrugated iron, pieces of rope and some old tent material. They were going to try to build a house for themselves. The mother was going to have another baby.

'Hello,' said the priest. 'What are you doing here? Well, never mind where you came from. You must have been sent to help us. We have to build a shelter quickly. If we don't, then this poor woman will be having her baby out in the rain.'

They all set to work. Other people brought hammers and nails and more wood and, after working hard for several hours, they had built a shelter which was dry inside and which the family could use as a home.

Not a moment too soon. The woman started to cry out. The priest rushed to fetch a nurse. There was no doctor or hospital in the shanty town.

The woman had her baby right there in the house Simon and Katie had helped to build. Simon and Katie waited in another house next door, and soon they could hear the tiny cries of the newborn child. Katie felt proud that she had been able to help to make the baby's arrival easier.

Most of the people could only speak in a language that was hard to understand, but Simon and Katie knew they were thanking them for helping.

The priest thanked them as well. 'I don't know where you two

After working hard for several hours, they had built a shelter which was dry inside and which the family could use as a home.

came from,' he said. 'It seemed to me you just dropped in from heaven.' He looked up, but all he could see was the Big Cloud. 'But you were a great help. I wish I had more helpers like you.'

Then he rushed away to comfort an old lady who was sick.

'When I grow up, I'm going to come back here and help all these poor people,' said Katie.

'Me too,' said Simon. He had forgotten about cricket and South Pole exploring.

Even though the Cloud had only just stopped crying, it had, in fact, helped the poor people a lot. There had been no rain for a long time, and the families were able to collect the freshwater tears that the Cloud sent splashing down and to drink them. They were crystal clear, much cleaner than the awful water which they had to fetch from a muddy well.

'I hope you get home all right,' shouted the priest as he dashed on his way to help someone else. 'Come and see us again soon.'

He would have been very surprised if he had seen the Cloud sending a piece of fluffy cloud (not too wet) down to collect Katie and Simon.

They floated back up to their comfortable, bouncy house. But neither of them felt hungry. They kept remembering seeing one little boy drinking a small bowl of bean soup, so thin that there were hardly any beans in it. They had thought that this was just the boy's lunch, but they had learned to their horror that this thin soup was all the boy would get to eat all day.

'When I'm president of the world,' said Simon fiercely, 'I shall see that all poor people have enough to eat and nice homes to live in.'

'Yes, and I'll send them all my pocket money,' said Katie.

They both felt very sad as they floated off northwards to New York, where they were going to have their final, but very exciting, adventure. But they would never forget the thin faces of the poor people of South America and they both hoped that, when they grew up, perhaps they could help them again.

CHAPTER 12

THE NEW YORK BANK RAID

The Cloud went ever so high up into the sky and sailed on over Mexico and the blue seas of the Caribbean until, one day, the children found themselves looking down on the wonderful city of New York.

New York is the city of skyscrapers: very tall buildings which really do seem to touch the sky. Many of them have forty or fifty floors and, as the Cloud came in quite low over the city, Simon and Katie found they were floating past office windows. The Cloud carefully arranged a route that meant they could watch the great city but no buildings would come sliding through.

The Cloud, of course, made itself as fluffy and delicate as possible so that it would not catch on the edges or spires of the buildings. But it also wanted to make itself look as nice as possible when viewed by the millions of people in the city below. This was the first time Katie realised that even clouds can be rather vain about the way they look.

The people inside the high offices rushed to their windows to see the children on the magic cloud and wave to them.

It was strange for Simon and Katie to have people up here on the same level as them. They had become used to being on their own, high above the seas and huge mountains. With, of course, only Timothy Tumbles to keep them company.

Timothy stood on the edge of the Cloud and barked joyfully to see a lot of people. What's the use of having people, he thought, if you don't bark at them?

Everyone looked so pleased to see them and so amazed that they were on the Cloud. One man leaned right out of a high window and shouted, 'Gee whiz, kiddiewinks. Happy sailing.'

Some people do talk rather like that in New York.

But New York, as well as being a city of tall, beautiful buildings, can also be a bad city. There are always a lot of robberies there.

As the Cloud was floating along over Fifth Avenue, which is the avenue with the most expensive shops in it, Simon, who was looking through his telescope, saw something sinister going on.

Two big black cars had drawn up outside a bank and some men had jumped out. They had masks on, and all carried guns.

The men rushed into the bank. Simon and Katie could hear the alarm bells begin to ring.

Only a moment later the men rushed out again, clutching bags that were evidently full of the money they had stolen. A policeman came up and shot at them with his gun, but the men shot back, and the cop fell to the ground with a bullet in his arm.

'Right,' said Simon, 'this is the most dangerous mission we've been on. Come on, Katie.' He raised his voice. 'Calling Cloud. Calling Cloud. Can you hear me?'

'With a shout like that,' retorted the Cloud, 'I could hear you if I were a hundred miles away.' (It wasn't cross. It was just making gentle fun of Simon, who had a rather piercing voice when he shouted.)

Simon was too excited to notice the Cloud teasing him. 'Please, Cloud, can you give us a super-high-powered cloudlet that will dive down very fast and be big enough to cover two big black cars?'

The Cloud felt rather sorry for teasing Simon when he was trying to help, so he acted very quickly. 'Cloud to Simon. Cloud to Simon,' he called, 'there is the cloudlet, right alongside. Hang on tight. It goes at a hundred miles an hour.'

Simon, Katie and Timothy Tumbles (*he* wasn't going to be left out) leapt onto the very sleek-looking cloudlet alongside. It was purring and buzzing with energy and power.

'Straight down, please,' yelled Simon. 'Hit those two black cars.'

They fairly hurtled through the air. Katie had not known the wind so strong since the adventure in Switzerland – or perhaps the South Pole. Anyway, she had to hang on tight herself, and grab hold of Timothy Tumbles, or he would have gone whizzing out into space.

It was like going into a dive on a fighter aircraft. Zoom-whizz. Whizz-zoom.

And then: howl. Screech. Scrunch. The cloudlet appeared to be applying its brakes violently. It screamed to a stop and, very neatly, covered the two cars into which the armed bandits were clambering.

The robbers were very puzzled. How had it happened that on a beautiful hot day in New York, they suddenly found their cars in the middle of a fog?

They began to rush about and fall into and out of their cars and fire their guns in all directions. Bullets seemed to be whizzing everywhere.

A peculiar thing had happened to Simon. Something he had not been expecting.

As he had leapt off the cloudlet when it had touched the ground, his eyes had been drawn, as if by some power beyond his control, towards two young children who stood huddled against the wall of the bank, trying to get out of the way of the bullets.

It was as if a funny kind of magic bleeper had started to go in his mind. He knew – just knew, without any doubt at all – that these two young children, dressed in jeans and white T-shirts, were brother and sister, and that they were the next brother and sister to take charge of the Big Cloud on which he and Katie had been travelling so long.

He could not have told you how he knew. He just knew. That is the way the changeover always happens.

Simon rushed across to the two children. 'Don't be afraid,' he yelled. 'Come and help me make sure the bandits can't get away.'

Timothy Tumbles rushed around, barking like mad as usual, and a bullet whizzed only half an inch above his tail.

Simon and Katie and their two newfound friends crept around the wheels of the robbers' cars and let all the air out of the tyres.

It was like going into a dive on a fighter aircraft.
Zoom-Whizz! Whizz-Zoom!

71

No one could see them because of the fog, which was really the cloudlet that had brought the children down.

Eventually the robbers got themselves into their cars and began to drive away. They had suddenly got the idea that the fog would enable them to sneak off without the police seeing them.

But they had two shocks coming to them.

Firstly, when they drove away, a strange sound came from the wheels. They went wobble-ti-bonk-crash, wobble-ti-bonk-crash. They were running on flat tyres.

Their second surprise was to find that in less than ten yards they had driven out of what they thought was a fog. And facing them, and behind them, and at the side of them – in fact, all round them – were New York cops.

The big policeman in charge of all the others shouted through a megaphone, 'Come out of the cars, you guys. Throw down your weapons. Anyone tries to make it out of here and we'll have him in cuffs before he can blink.'

All the robbers gave in. It was hopeless for them.

The big policeman shouted through the megaphone again, 'I sure would like to meet the people who let those tyres down. I want to thank them.'

Simon and Katie and Timothy Tumbles found themselves standing before him. And at their side were their two new friends, who told them they were called Johnnie and Susannah.

Not long after, the big detective took all four of the youngsters and Timothy to the office of the Mayor of New York. Television cameras whirred. And, in front of millions of viewers, all the children – and Timothy – were presented by the Mayor with bravery awards for the prevention of crime.

They walked back together along Fifth Avenue. A crowd full of curiosity was still gathered around the cloudlet that had come down on such a sunny day. As soon as it saw Simon, the cloudlet began to buzz and whir, getting ready for take-off.

Johnnie and Susannah looked as if they were going to say goodbye.

'Oh no,' said Simon, smiling, 'I haven't had time to tell you yet.

But you two have been chosen to be the Cloud Children and to take charge of the magic cloud up there.'

'The what children?' asked Johnnie. He was so amazed he could hardly speak.

To Simon it sounded just like himself asking the question of the boy, Sam, all that time ago in England when he and Katie had first gone aboard the Cloud. 'I don't know how I know it, but I just do,' he said to Johnnie. 'I know I have to ask you and your sister to be the Cloud Children on our cloud for the next year.'

'For a year?' yelled Johnnie. 'We can't go away for a year. My mom would lose it if we were even late for supper.'

And so, of course, Simon had to try to explain to Johnnie and Susannah about the wonderful cloud. He told them about the Secret Army of Children who were sailing around the world which badly needed good things done, and that, although it might seem like a year while you were riding on it, the Cloud delivered you back at your home at the very same second that you had sailed off on it. In time for supper, in fact.

Once they had asked all their questions, Johnnie and Susannah were filled with the spirit of adventure. They did both ask, 'What are we going to eat?' But Simon and Katie were able to reassure them that they would get some good food as soon as they reached the Cloud.

'Jump on,' Simon called.

Johnnie and Susannah had looks of doubt on their faces as they jumped on the cloudlet. They thought they might drop right through it.

'Simon to cloudlet. Simon to cloudlet,' Simon called.

'Cloudlet responding. Cloudlet responding. Over.'

'Full speed back to the Big Cloud, please, cloudlet,' shouted Simon.

And – whoosh – off they went. The elegant Americans shopping on Fifth Avenue that day had never been so surprised in all their lives.

'I wonder where I could buy one of those clouds,' said a rich woman.

73

But, of course, you cannot buy magic clouds. And only children can ride on them.

Johnnie and Susannah were very cautious at first. But, once they had got aboard and had a good bounce around in the sunshine on the Big Cloud, and once they had had some chocolate-vanilla-strawberry gateau which Simon fetched for them from the Cloud's cake department: once those things had happened, they were very content and happy.

'I never knew a cloud could be such a ding-dong smasheroo!' yelled Johnnie as he bounced.

Simon and Katie agreed they would have to get used to Johnnie's American expressions.

They were all so tired they settled down together under the cloud blanket with Timothy Tumbles on top. There they snoozed away as the Cloud drifted out across the great Atlantic on its way to Simon and Katie's home.

Epilogue

BACK HOME IN TIME FOR TEA

The great Cloud rushed across the Atlantic. It obviously did not want to be a second late in getting Simon and Katie home for their tea. Which, of course, would be at the same time as they had left. A very complicated and clever thing for a cloud to do.

Down below, speeding past, was the mighty Atlantic Ocean with white crests on its huge waves.

Simon and Katie made great friends with Johnnie and Susannah during the trip. Johnnie told them that he and his sister lived in what he called a tenement house in New York. It was rather a poor area, and many families lived in flats in the same block. But it was their home and they liked it.

Johnnie and Susannah loved their mother, but, unfortunately, their father had died. So Mom, as Johnnie called her, did some cleaning to make money. There were two other sisters and a small brother.

Simon said, 'We've met an Arab boy, a French brother and sister, some Indian people, some South American people – and now a boy and girl from New York. It's been super.'

'Sure has been great to meet you,' said Johnnie.

'Sure has, honey,' said Susannah.

Simon liked being called 'honey'. It was very friendly, and it made him feel happy. It even made him feel a bit soppy towards his sister. He gave Katie a squeeze.

Katie felt all sad now that it was coming to the time when they would have to leave the Cloud.

The Cloud floated over the English coast.

Simon put a cloud telescope to his eye. 'Soon be home now, Katie,' he shouted. 'I can see our house.' Then he added, 'Oh, yes, and I can see Mum at the door.'

Katie had a look. There was their mother leaning out of the door of the house where they lived.

Katie put the tube to her ear. She heard her mother calling, 'Katie, Simon! Where are you? It's tea time.'

'Oh, I'm so happy,' Katie said, 'and yet so sad.'

She burst into tears and kissed both Johnnie and Susannah. Johnnie was quite embarrassed.

Simon was the perfect gentleman. He shook hands.

They fashioned a cloud parachute and basket and stepped in. Timothy Tumbles hopped in too.

'Goodbye, Cloud,' Simon and Katie called. 'Thank you ever so much for looking after us so well.'

Katie could have sworn she heard a big sob from the SECRET area in the middle. The Cloud was always like this when children left it. It was very soft-hearted really.

Then the Cloud shouted, 'Goodbye, children. Thank you for doing all the good things you've done. I'll drop down to see you now and again as I go round the world.'

In a few moments, the two children were down on the ground in their own garden and their parachute had been sent off to rejoin the Cloud. They could see two small, grinning faces peering at them over the edge of the Cloud, then four waving hands, and the Cloud was drifting away, getting smaller and smaller.

'Oh, there you are, children. I wondered where you were. Up to mischief, I suppose. Your tea's ready. Come along.' It was their mother's voice.

Simon whispered, 'My watch has begun to tick again. We're back in ordinary time.'

Katie was more worried about Timothy Tumbles. 'I wonder what Mummy is going to say when she knows we've got a dog,' she said nervously.

Timothy Tumbles solved the problem for them without any trouble. As soon as he got inside the house, he dashed up to Katie's

They could see two small, grinning faces peering at them over the edge of the Cloud; then four waving hands and the Cloud was drifting away getting smaller and smaller.

mother and made such a great fuss of her that no one could refuse to give him a home. Dogs are very intelligent animals, you know.

'It doesn't seem a moment since we were in the field, does it?' said Katie, wistfully.

'Well, I don't suppose it is, dear,' said their mother.

'It was exciting, wasn't it?' said Katie.

'Sure was,' said Simon, forgetting himself and using one of Johnnie's phrases.

'You sound like an American, dear,' said their mother. 'I suppose it's all the television you watch. You had an exciting time? What were you up to?'

'Oh, just floating about. Looking at this and that,' said Simon before Katie could give the game away.

'Oh,' said their mum. 'Well, that sounds nice. So long as you weren't floating too high in the sky.'

She laughed at her little joke.

After tea, Simon, Katie and Timothy Tumbles went out into the garden. They could not see the Cloud any more, which made them feel sad. But, at the same time, their mother had said they could keep Timothy Tumbles if no one claimed him, and that made them happy. So they were happy-sad.

Simon grinned. 'I'll bet Susannah and Johnnie have a super time,' he said.

'Yes, I'll bet they do,' sighed Katie. 'Just think of all that cloud ice cream to eat.'

They both looked up at the sky. Perhaps one day they would see their cloud again, and Ali Abu, Pierre and Sophie and Susannah and Johnnie. And perhaps someday they could help the poor children of India and South America some more.

It all seemed to have been too magical to be true.

But then little Timothy Tumbles jumped up and gave them each a kiss and a wag. He was there with them, wasn't he?

So it must all have been true.

Lightning Source UK Ltd.
Milton Keynes UK
UKHW041352150121
377059UK00004B/218